A Final Request For Mercy

AMY LAURENS

OTHER WORKS

SANCTUARY SERIES

Where Shadows Rise
Through Roads Between
When Worlds Collide

KADITEOS SERIES

How Not To Acquire A Castle
How Not To Ring The Hero's Bell (2019)
How Not To Take Over The World (2019)

SHORT STORY COLLECTIONS

Of Sea Foam and Blood
Darkness and Good

NON-FICTION

How To Write Dogs
How To Theme
How To Create Cultures

Find other works by the author at
www.amylaurens.com

A Final Request For Mercy

INKLET #8

AMY LAURENS

Inkprint
PRESS
www.inkprintpress.com

Print ISBN: 978-1-925825-00-8
eBook ISBN: 9781386997559

www.inkprintpress.com

*National Library of Australia Cataloguing-in-Publication
Data*
Laurens, Amy 1985 –
A Final Request For Mercy
46 p.
ISBN: 978-1-925825-00-8
Inkprint Press, Canberra, Australia
1. Fiction—Animals 2. Fiction—Short Stories 3.
Fiction—Friendship

First Print Edition: April 2019
Cover design © Inkprint Press
Interior art © Heather Craik

A FINAL REQUEST
FOR MERCY

THE FULL MOON SHONE, BATHING THE yard in muted silver and turning Abbi into a dark, doggy shadow as she lay underneath the lemon tree. She stretched, tail thumping the ground; the night was warm, the Zac rabbit was home, and all was well with the world.

A movement caught her ear and she raised her muzzle to sniff. Algernon the guinea pig, appearing for a midnight snack in the cage across the yard. His head bobbed as he ate, ears flapping and lettuce crunch-crunching in his teeth.

The tip of Abbi's tail twitched. Chasing him around his cage never failed to amuse her—especially since he never failed to run.

Abbi sat up and scratched at her collar, which always managed to tickle the itchy spot under her chin. A good chase would help her forget the discomfort.

A soft moan made her ears prick high—but Algernon munched away as though nothing was wrong. Strange.

Abbi sauntered over to the hutch. "Hey, piggy-pig. What's up?"

Algernon ignored her, concentrating on his food.

Another moan.

Abbi's eyebrows twitched. "Zac?" she asked. "Is that you?" She lowered her head against the hutch, listening for the rabbit's presence. He mostly kept himself inside at nights, especially now the frosts were here—but moaning was new.

Another moan, and a rustle of straw. She pressed closer. "Zac?"

Zac's reply was so soft Abbi couldn't make out the words.

"Zac, is everything all right?"

Another faint response, almost beyond hearing. "Come here."

"I am here." She snuffed through the corner of the cage. "See?"

"Open... Open the lid."

Abbi started. "What?" she said. "It sounded like you said 'Open the lid'."

"Yes."

"What? No! I can't do that." She nodded towards the house. "They'd kill me."

"Please?"

"Why?"

"I... need you."

Abbi stared at the house, sleeping quietly in the night. She scratched at her ear, pondering. "I suppose so. If you really *need* me..."

"I do," Zac panted.

Abbi sighed. *Here goes nothing.* She leapt onto the roof of the cage where three bricks held down the lid. She shoved at one with her nose and it scraped a few centimetres. She shoved again and it toppled off, landing with a thunk. The other two followed, then she jumped back to the ground. She nibbled at the lid, trying to get a good grip.

"Please hurry."

Abbi tugged and the lid opened. She swallowed, half expecting one of the girls to burst out of the house and yell at her. But the house slept. She stuck her nose into the cage.

In the moonlight, the rabbit was nothing more than a silvery bump in a corner. Abbi twitched her nose; he smelled wrong. "Are you okay, Zac?"

The silvery mound shivered—Zac inched his head around to face her.

Abbi winced, sensing the effort that the simple movement took.

"No," he said in response to her question. "I'm not."

"What... what's wrong?"

Zac shuddered. "Die... dying."

Abbi jerked away. No. Zac had been sick, but that was before. He was better now. He couldn't be dying.

"Abbi?"

Her nose trembled. "I'm here."

"I... I want you to do me a favour."

"Zac, you're not dying, don't be silly. The girls will make you better, they fixed you last time—"

"No." His whisper was faint, so faint—but firm. Abbi shivered. "I didn't get better last time."

Abbi pawed at the ground. "What do you mean? You were running around like anything last week. They fixed you, the girls fixed you, they *did*."

Zac shook his head. "They didn't," he said. "Not forever. It's... it's come back, and this time... The vet couldn't help me. I can't beat it."

His head lolled against the straw and adrenalin flushed Abbi's system. "No, Zac!" His sides filled out again, and she breathed.

"I'm sorry," he said.

Abbi chest constricted, and she nudged him. "You can," she said. "Please, you can beat it." But the acrid scent of his illness crept into her nostrils, faint but inexorable, and deep inside she knew Zac was right.

"You smell it," he said, and she nodded. He drew a faltering breath. "I want you to end it."

Abbi leapt back, hackles raised, growling. "No! I won't do it."

Silence. Abbi crept back to the cage.

"Never… never mind." Zac flicked his vein-webbed ear, brushing it over Abbi's cheek.

She drew in a lungful of sick air, staring at him with misting eyes. Pain. She could smell it, all over him. He was right: he was dying.

"Just take me out," he said. "Let me… let me get out one last time."

She nudged him softly. "Okay."

For a moment she stood still, nose buried in the softness of his fur, feeling his heart beat against her and his breath shudder through his body. A queasy jolt ran through her stomach. "Zac, I can't do what you want. I can't."

Zac looked at her with somber eyes. "You will," he said. "When the time comes, you won't be able to stop yourself."

Abbi shifted, uneasy. "I'm sorry. I can't take you out of your cage after all. Not if that's what you want."

"Abbi, please. I… It hurts. I just want to feel the grass one last time."

She squeezed her eyes shut, but she couldn't block out the smell. She sighed. One quick run on the grass wouldn't hurt. Then she could just put him back in his cage, and everything would be fine.

Zac shuddered, whiskers tickling Abbi's nose.

She took him gently by the scruff of his neck.

Slowly, she eased him up, lifted him out of the cage, and placed him on the ground. She sat next to him and looked around the yard. The moonlight cast everything into relief, sharpening the edges, all black or silver.

Abbi glanced at Zac, shivering even though the night was warm. His fur glistened. She gave a half smile. Silver-furred rabbit and shadow-haired dog—together, they were the night.

She watched Zac out of the corner of her eye, wondering if perhaps he'd accepted her earlier response. Would he try to convince her? He sat with the air of someone waiting. But that might be nothing; he was probably working up the energy for one last tour of the yard.

And then, without warning, he leapt. Two feet up in the air, he bucked. He landed and sprinted down the yard, a silver blur in the half-light.

Abbi leapt to her feet in an instant, instinct in overdrive. It ran. *Chase. Chase!*

The blur was fast, but she was faster. *Chase! Catch!* She was the hunter and the prey would not escape.

Black paws flashed as she gained ground, step after step—and then she was on it. She reached it and teeth closed around fur, drew shut with a crunch. She lifted the furry mop and shook.

Prey. Caught it. She grinned, dropping the silver bundle on the ground. She sniffed at it, nudged it, bumped it, turned it over.

An eye caught the light.

Abbi's legs collapsed underneath her. "No," she said as she crumbled to the ground. "Zac!" She nuzzled the rabbit's soft stomach. "Zac-bunny, Zac, please, I'm sorry! I didn't mean it!"

But he didn't move.

She whimpered. "No." A howl rose in her throat and she lifted her nose to the sky. "Aroo! Arooooo!"

The neighbouring dogs took up her cry, sensing something amiss. Howls echoed through the night, a dirge, and a lament for what she had done.

It's his fault! she thought angrily. *He knew I'd chase if he ran! It's not my fault I'm a dog!* But the guilt still gnawed at her stomach.

Abbi rested her head on Zac's body. "I'm so sorry."

The body grew cold beneath her chin. She rose and lifted him in her mouth, gentle, as though he might break. She padded across the grass, slowly, deliberately, a funeral procession of one. She laid him back on the straw of the hutch and climbed in beside him. She curled up, her body shielding his, black and silver together in the black and silver night.

"Goodnight, Zac," she said, and wept.

THE MAKING OF
A FINAL REQUEST FOR MERCY

Liana always accuses me of writing dark tragedies, and usually I disagree. Usually, there is a hopeful ending that prevents the story from being characterised as a true tragedy.

This story, however, is as close to a true tragedy as I've ever written. Usually, I vastly prefer hopeful endings, but this time, my hand was forced: the ending was chosen for me.

Because, you see, this is a true story.

Oh, I don't mean the specifics of it, of course, the interactions and verbalisations between dog and bunny. But the fact of the matter is, my sisters once had a silver-grey bunny called Zac, and a black Labrador puppy called Abbi, and one morning they went out to the to discover that Abbi had broken in the roof of the rabbit hutch, and the rabbit was no more.

My babiest sister wasn't even in double digits yet. The least I could do was write a story that attempted to rationalise what had happened, to suggest that maybe, just maybe, it wasn't the senseless tragedy it appeared to be.

DOWNLOAD YOUR FREE EBOOK

When you buy a print book from Inkprint Press, we like to say THANK YOU by offering you the ebook for free!

Please head to www.inkprintpress.com/inklets/8/ and the use the coupon 8INKLET to get your copy of this Inklet in epub AND mobi today!
(Coupon will only work once.)

Read more by Amy Laurens!

WHERE SHADOWS RISE

CHAPTER ONE

THE DOORBELL RANG. That doesn't sound exciting in and of itself, but let me assure you: it was the most heart-pounding thing to happen all week. It was my birthday, I was home alone, and because of the stupid witness protection business, I'd been stuck in the house all summer. I hadn't even been allowed out to see friends, because we'd arrived in town at the end of last year with only three school weeks to go—so I didn't have any friends.

Well. I had friends, but they were back in Melbourne, and I wasn't allowed to contact them for fear someone would track down our new location. Lucky me.

Anyway, it was my birthday, I was alone because Mum and Dad had gone to do something regarding birthday surprises and Anna had inexplicably chosen to go with them, and the doorbell had just rung. I stared at the closed door, heart pounding, while our chocolate Labrador, Veve, tried to chew it down. Was I going to open it?

Of course I was going to open it. The chances of it being a mobster were slim to none; for starters, a mobster wouldn't have rung the bell.

I opened it.

"Miss Tanning?" The deliveryman raised a questioning eyebrow and cocked a digital pen at me.

I nodded, heart flip-flopping, and scrawled a fair impersonation of my signature on the digital pad.

He handed over a small, brown-paper parcel with a handwritten address, and departed.

I closed the door behind him, throat dry, and stared down at Veve. On the one hand, yay birthday present. On the other, holy crap, someone had our address. That was *not* a good thing.

It became even less of a good thing when I noticed that the parcel was indeed addressed to a Miss Tanning: a Miss *Anna* Tanning, as in my sister, not me, Emma Tanning.

Anger bubbled up in my chest, hot and tight, and the parcel protested in my grip.

Veve whined softly.

"How could she *do* this?" I whispered to Veve.

I turned the parcel over. It was from Kade, Anna's frogging ex-boyfriend. Who apparently wasn't an 'ex' after all.

Urgh. I ground my teeth. "You know what?" I asked Veve.

She looked up at me with her liquid brown eyes, tongue lolling as she smiled.

"Screw it. If Anna can get interstate mail from people who aren't even supposed to know we exist anymore, you and I can go for a walk on my birthday. What do you think?"

They say dogs don't speak English, but Veve sure as heck knew the word 'walk'—though I think in her vocabulary it was something closer to 'Magical Trip To Disneyland' and less like 'Comparatively Bland Meander Through Trees'.

She tucked her tail right under her butt and shot down the hall, whirling in frantic circles a few times at the end before pelting back as I retrieved her lead from the drawer in the front cabinet.

I rolled my eyes as I clipped her lead onto her collar. For my troubles, I got slimed right up the nostrils. "You're disgusting, you know that?" I wiped off the worst of the dog slobber on the shoulder of my shirt. She just grinned.

Out on the street, she leapt and twisted madly. "Hair-brain," I told her, snapping the lead to get her attention. "It's just a walk."

She just snorted—and stiffened. I followed her gaze to where a flock of corellas pecked their way through the dry grass at the end of the street.

"Veve!"

My shout was in vain: the lead burned through my fingers and Veve shot down the road, a chocolate bullet howling death and destruction for all things feathered.

I cursed her to the lower circles of doggie hell. Which probably involved, I don't know, a world devoid of birds, cats, people, sunshine, and walks, if Veve was anything to go by.

"Veve!" If the sight of the mad Lab-rat barrelling toward them hadn't scared the birds off, my shouts would have. "Come back here *now!*"

Predictably, she ignored me, pounding down the slope, through the fringe of gum trees, and down the narrow stairs between giant granite boulders that led to the river.

"Stupid frogging brainless beast of a stupid frogging dog," I muttered as I followed. "If Mum gets home before we do and freaks out, I swear, I'll pluck your tail hairs out."

Empty threats, obviously, but Mum's freak-out wouldn't be. Her thoughts would go straight to the day Anna nearly died—and I wouldn't blame her.

I should have left a note. Urgh.

The stairs ended and I found myself on a track broad enough for two twisting along a creek the colour of bitter tea. Tussock grass clustered in spikes—where the eucalypts would let it—and hot summer sunlight glinted from the leaves. Somewhere to my right, downstream and in the opposite direction to the house, Veve barked. I exhaled like a whale coming up for air and set out after her.

Veve bounded out from the under-growth in front of me, a dolphin leaping through water, tongue flapping with every bound. "Stupid mutt," I told her under my breath.

She didn't care what I thought (of course), and saved a leap for the last minute so she could plant muddy feet on my hips as I tried to catch her collar.

I straightened, about to insult her some more, and realised that she'd gone stiff again, ears pricked and mouth tight, listening down the path.

My neck prickled. Someone was coming. A second later, I heard footsteps in the gravel, and a low, male voice, humming, or maybe singing softly.

My chest constricted, and just as suddenly my hands were slick. Chances were it was just a stranger out for a midday stroll, but my stomach wound knots about my memories and

I smelled the hot concrete and melting asphalt, old oil and stale urine of the Lilydale train station where the body had been hidden in a toilet stall, the body of the girl who'd looked like Anna.

I had to get off the path.

"Come on, Veve," I said, pulling her close, white-knuckled as I stepped into the undergrowth. The tea tree scrub protested, but I shoved my way through anyway, glancing over my shoulder as the humming grew louder.

I kept going until I couldn't hear footsteps any more, until the wind swallowed the hum that sounded too like the warning cry of a hive—danger, we're working here, come close and get stung. I didn't want to get stung; visions of a blood-streaked face refused to be blinked away.

Only Veve tugging brought me back to myself, and I realised firstly that I was holding the lead way too tight, cutting off Veve's air supply, secondly that the reason my cheeks were suddenly cold was because I'd been crying, and thirdly that I'd found the creek again, looping back parallel maybe fifty meters or so from the path.

Abruptly, I dropped Veve's lead and strode forward to kneel by the water. I dipped my hands in. A shiver slid through me at its chill, and I scooped it up to wash my face.

Flinging the excess water away, I gulped at the air, deep, calming breaths all the way down into my belly, and visualised a river washing away the blood from my thoughts, just like the police psych had taught me.

Once the space behind my eyes was calm and black, I drew in one last forceful breath, and opened my eyes. Perched on a rock by the creek, I hugged my knees to my chest as cool water lapped at my toes. Veve was a little upstream, just before the creek bent back toward the path, doggy paddling in circles in a deep spot where the water broadened to maybe ten meters across. In front of me it was broad but shallow, only ankle deep, its path torn to white foam by the rocks.

And—I gasped. In the middle of the stream, glittering in the sun like a piece of fallen sky, was the hugest butterfly I'd ever seen.

Which was pretty huge; besides the fact that I grew up visiting the Melbourne Zoo with its impressive butterfly house every Christmas since I could remember, Mum and Dad had taken us up to Brisbane for a family holiday two years ago, and we'd seen giant tropical butterflies bigger than my hand.

This one, bright blue with black edging like a Ulysses, was bigger than both my hands put together.

And then it turned around.

Okay. I'd grown up reading fairy tales as much as the next person, and although I'd had a horse-crazy stage instead of a fairy-crazy stage like Anna had, I'd seen all her paraphernalia.

Still, none of it prepared me for finding something that looked exactly like a fairy, standing smack in the middle of a creek in boring, back-water Nowra.

I'm pretty sure my eyes were only hanging in their sockets by a thread.

And then it talked.

Her face lit up like a cloud had just uncovered the sun as she spotted me. "Hi there!" she said, fluttering over.

I just stared, heart pounding against my ribcage as though it wanted to run away from the absurdity of it all. "No," I said. "I'm hallucinating."

The fairy frowned. "I don't think so."

I shook my head. "No. No, things like this do not happen. Things like this aren't *real*." I stood, backing up a step.

The fairy sighed. "I promise. I'm quite real."

"You would say that, wouldn't you," I said, eyeing her. "Veve!" I waved at the dog and hopped from one foot to the other, trying to lure her in with the promise of play. "We're going now!"

Veve, adorable beast that she was, landed a little upstream and shook vigorously before trotting toward me. I backed hurriedly away from the bank, dancing to keep Veve's attention.

"Wait!" the fairy cried, wings snapping out and propelling her a couple of feet into the air. "You're a Traveller! I need to talk to you!"

"Uh huh, sure," I said as I wound the lead around my hand and set off back into the bushes. This was punishment for leaving the house, obviously. The universe was out to get me, reminding me forcefully that once you started disregarding some rules, who knew what other rules you'd end up flouting.

The rules of physics, for example.

I glanced back once, right before the bushes hid the stream altogether. Blue flashed, high up, but I ducked to get a better view and it was only the sky. I scowled. Stupid fairy. Stupid universe. Served me right for leaving the house in the first place. Urgh. "Come on, Veve," I said, snapping the lead. "Even if the house is prison, at least it's *sane*."

I was stomping so furiously as I burst out onto the path that when a figure rose from a stoop only a couple of steps away, I squeaked in surprise.

I scowled. People rarely surprised me; usually I could tell without trying that someone was near. I really must have been off in my own little world.

I glowered at the boy who lived to make my school life a misery. "What are you doing here?" I snapped. "Isn't it bad enough that I have to deal with you on school days? Which, by the way, don't start until tomorrow. You're ruining my holidays."

Okay, so maybe that was a little harsh, but come on. It was *Scott*. I'd arrived in town with three weeks left in the school year, and he'd spent every day of them humiliating me in front of his mates, and I didn't care for a repeat this year.

Scott eyed me warily, which was a strange expression on him.

Usually he strode around like he knew without a doubt that he was too good for the world, and also—somewhere deeper, somewhere I'd only caught a glimpse of once or twice— that it had nothing left to throw at him that could hurt.

Occasionally, in my more generous moments, I wondered what had happened to make him look that way.

Mostly, however, I just wondered why he was such a moron.

"What are you doing here?" he asked, voice dripping with accusation and suspicion.

My hands fisted of their own accord, and beside me Veve's hackles rose as she chimed in with a low-pitched, rumbling growl. I flicked the free end of the lead at her nose. "Nothing," I said, in a rousing blaze of wit. "What are you doing?"

He scowled. "You shouldn't be here."

For one heart-stopping instant I thought he meant out here generally, walking around, as if he knew what had happened and why I'd hidden away all summer. Then I realised he was nodding into the undergrowth. I rolled my eyes. "I might be a city slicker," I bit off, "but I'm not stupid. I made enough noise to scare off a herd of elephants, let alone any snakes that might have been lying around." The thought chilled me, though; I *hadn't* been thinking about snakes when I'd hurried off the path. One badly-timed footstep and a brown snake bite later, and I could be a dead body too.

But Scott had moved on, stalking off down the path. He had nice shoulders, I'd give him that much. Pity he couldn't derive his personality from them, instead of whatever dead weight it was he kept inside his head for brains.

Beside me, Veve growled again, louder this time, more urgent. I snapped the lead at her and stared after Scott's retreating form, trying to think of something cutting.

It was only when Veve growled for the third time that I realised she wasn't even facing Scott. Instead, she was looking back into the bushes—and something dark was flickering in there, deep in the shadows of the trees.

My chest squeezed in on itself and adrenalin shot through my body. Veve's growling grew louder until it broke in a bark, something midway between slavering and terrified, and I realised my tongue was stuck to the roof of my mouth. Carefully I peeled it away, unable to tear my eyes from the shifting darkness in the bushes. There was no discernible form, just shadow, darker than it should have been this soon after midday, and a pervasive sense of dread clamping down on me like an on-coming storm.

Veve began backing away, hackles prickling, growl rising and falling like thunder. I glanced down at her, back to the shadows—and they were closer, much closer than they had been.

I turned and bolted.

Keep reading! Head to
http://www.amylaurens.com/book
s/sanctuary/where-shadows-rise/
to buy your copy now!

ABOUT THE AUTHOR

AMY LAURENS is an Australian author of fantasy fiction for all ages. She has never seen a fairy or travelled to Sanctuary (sadly), but she has definitely owned a Labrador almost exactly like Veve (though Amy's Labrador was yellow, not brown).

In addition to the *Sanctuary* series of portal fantasy stories set in Nowra, Australia, Amy has written the humorous fantasy series *Kaditeos: Mercury*, beginning with *How Not To Acquire A Castle*, as well as a whole bunch of nonfiction for writers and non-writers alike.

You can find out more about Amy at her website, www.amylaurens.com.

INKLETS

Collect them all! Released on the 1st and 15th of each month.

INKLET #007
SEVENTY
LIANA BROOKS

INKLET #008
A Final Request for Mercy
AMY LAURENS

INKLET #009
the kitten psychologist vs. the kitten's owners
THEA VAN DIEPEN

INKLET #010
Answer the Question
AMY LAURENS

INKLET #011
Happily, Red
AMY LAURENS

INKLET #012
the kitten psychologist tries to be patient through email
THEA VAN DIEPEN

INKLET #013
DRAGON Tuesday
AMY LAURENS

INKLET #014
RED PLANET REFUGEES
LIANA BROOKS

INKLET #015
the kitten psychologist & What The Kitten Did
THEA VAN DIEPEN

Cherry
Blossom
AMY LAURENS

Alone
AMY LAURENS

the kitten psychologist
& The Kitten
Come To A Conclusion
THEA VAN DIEPEN

LEVEL NINE
LIANA BROOKS

To Dust
AMY LAURENS

Interchange
AMY LAURENS

Emalia's
Lanterns
LIANA BROOKS

Dear Santa
AMY LAURENS

The
Quilt-Maker's
Scrap
AMY LAURENS